# WE HAVE ALWAYS LIVED IN THE BREAK ROOM

## MICHAEL ALLEN ROSE

Copyright © 2023 by Michael Allen Rose

All rights reserved.

No part of this book may be reproduced or transmitted in any form or by any means, electronic or mechanical, except for the purpose of review and/or reference, without explicit permission in writing from the publisher.

Cover design copyright © 2023 by Kelley York
*sleepyfoxstudio.net*

Published by Water Dragon Publishing
*waterdragonpublishing.com*

ISBN 978-1-959804-80-2 (Trade Paperback)

FIRST EDITION

10 9 8 7 6 5 4 3 2 1

*To Sauda,
who keeps me sane, even during apocalypses.
You guide me to the window.*

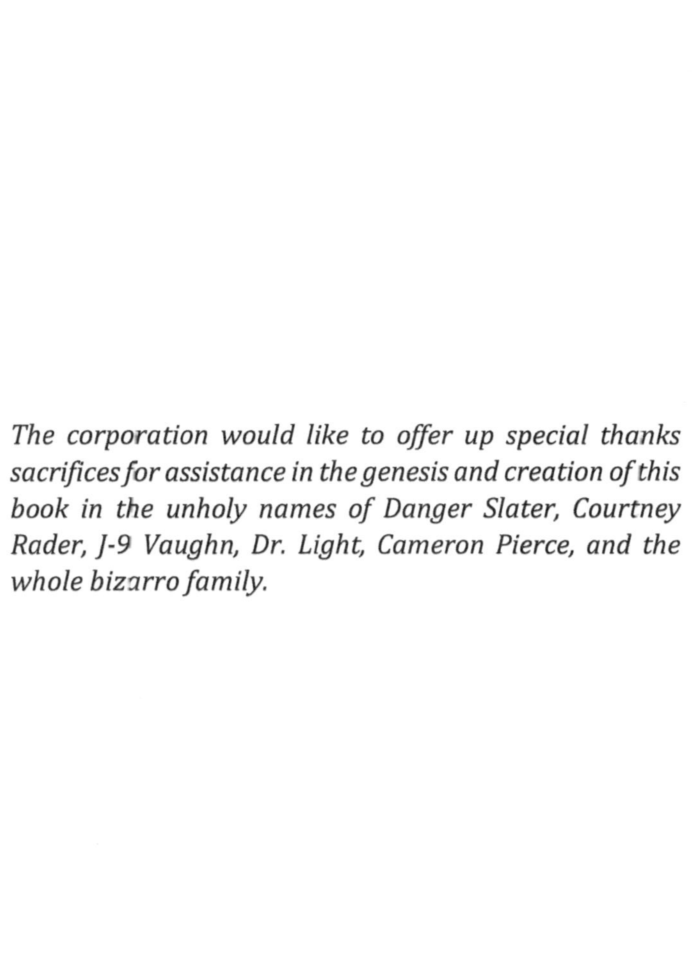

*The corporation would like to offer up special thanks sacrifices for assistance in the genesis and creation of this book in the unholy names of Danger Slater, Courtney Rader, J-9 Vaughn, Dr. Light, Cameron Pierce, and the whole bizarro family.*

# WE HAVE ALWAYS LIVED IN THE BREAK ROOM

W AHL'TER DINSDALE typed the last line of data into his spreadsheet, zoning out to the mechanical clicks of keyboards and the ambient hum of his computer. He scratched idly in the traditional way at his traditional loincloth, letting his fingertips graze over the traditional naugahyde from which it was crafted.

He had skinned the break-room couch himself, on his sixteenth birthday. It was the traditional way to mark the passage to manhood for his tribe, those of the break-room. As long back as anyone could find words to tell, boys of the break-room would sneak into the northwest corner at the time of only security lights, when the fluorescent flicker was turned low, and the night-watch howled their patrol, echoes in the distant corridors. They would creep silently to the break-room couch, slipping past untamed and feral interns.

The boy would take his finest wooden ruler, with a steel straight edge, honed to razor-sharp perfection. He would find a seam at sofa's edge, and without a sound, he would slide the edge underneath. Only the most skilled could split the threads without spilling forth the stuffing within. The break-room couch had much difficulty healing from a deeper wound, where the polyester and foam bled out. A delicate and precise operation was best. This was good in the eyes of the managers.

When Wahl'ter's time had come, he had been skilled indeed. His skinning was heralded as a good omen, a prophecy of greatness. The couch had healed and re-grown its skin nearly overnight. The layer Wahl'ter had sliced was perfectly thin and flat, like deli meat from the sacred cafeteria, and he had decided to form it into a loincloth so all others would understand his place in the tribe.

This was why he was a master accountant for the tribe of the break-room. This was why he wore the polka-dotted tie.

Wahl'ter stood and surveyed the break-room proper. The usual mix of folks walked briskly to and fro, doing their various daily duties. Bertram the Train-or, Train-or of interns, stood proudly atop a cola vending machine, barking orders at a herd of interns below. The interns, three girls and two boys, rushed about, scrambling to show how well trained they were. Their leashes pulled taut with friction as they wove in and out of one another's paths, like they were taking part in a dance to music only they could hear. It certainly couldn't be the slow and subtle cadence of the day muzak, which piped in from above, dribbling gentle melodies of productivity on the tribe.

Bertram the Train-or pointed sharply at the doorway, into the great hallway beyond, and addressed his herd: "Interns! You will find the Anderson file! He or she of you who first finds the Anderson file, they shall be dealt a great boon!" With a flourish, Bertram the Train-or reached into the pocket of his chinos and pulled forth a printed coupon. The interns hooted and hollered at the sight of it, stomping their feet and clapping their hands. "Settle down, lest none of you earn this! Now, hear me well: the first to find the Anderson file shall receive this gift. Behold, the commendation!"

The words "Intern of the Month" shone in sparkling gold letters, lending an air of authentic magic to the humble paper on which it was printed. This was a special reward indeed, for the metallic ink was kept sacred, and guarded fiercely by the covetous witches of the secretarial pool. Bertram the Train-or must have traded something dear indeed to gain access to the metallic inks.

Wahl'ter had once attained some puff paint, and shuddered at the thought of all the boxes of paper clips he had sacrificed to the witches for but a single tube. It was worth it, however. He glanced up at his nameplate, hung over his desk, and smiled at the sight of his name in puffy neon lettering. Wahl'ter Dinsdale was not an ostentatious man, but he understood well the prestige of his position in the tribe, and how appearances mattered. The Dinsdale lineage carried Duplicate of New Author (template) with it an aura, built from effort and care over generations, radiating beyond even the furthest reaches of the financial department.

Bertram the Train-or brought the certificate down to waist level, and howled out a battle cry. "Friday is coming! Now, march!" He let the interns off their leashes with three quick snaps.

With a shout, the pack of interns bounded from the room, heading off toward parts unknown to begin their search. Bertram the Train-or hopped down from his perch and grinned at Wahl'ter. Wahl'ter returned the smile, and held out his hand. They shook, in the traditional way. There was no need for a business card exchange. Wahl'ter and Bertram the Train-or could greet each other informally without losing status, as they had been colleagues since they were young.

"Hail, Bertram the Train-or. A fine herd of interns, this crew."

"Aye, Wahl'ter, I have done my best in their training. Soon, I believe they shall be ready to join us and find their place in the office."

"Do you think they'll stay?"

Bertram the Train-or looked around at the many vending machines, and the comfortable furniture that always grew back its upholstery. He nodded at the automatic coffee maker, and the many packets of sugar. "If they have brains in their heads, they'll stay. For, who could want anything finer than the break-room? Here, the food is plentiful. The water, it flows from the indoor plumbing. We have many places to sit, even sofas, and are not defined by our rolling chairs as they are in other lands. Truly, we lead lives of abundance."

"Aye, true." Wahl'ter shook his head, as the corners of his mouth turned to a grimace. "I worry, though. I have heard rumors."

"Rumors?"

"Around the great water cooler, where all the tribal elders gather. There has been talk." Wahl'ter looked around to make sure none of the younger break-room tribe members were lingering nearby. There was no need to frighten them. Not just yet. "Some say the time of layoffs is coming."

Bertram the Train-or stared at his friend for a moment, then suddenly snorted with laughter. "Surely, you are a Dil-b'hert! Your joke is hilarious! I would like to make a photocopy of it for my cubicle wall so as to never forget this moment."

Wahl'ter straightened his tie, and Bertram the Train-or stopped laughing, worry creeping into his eyes. "I tell you, perhaps it is all a jest. Perhaps, as the managers say, you don't have to be crazy to work here, but it helps. But, what if the layoffs do come? Will our candy bars remain stocked? Will there still be cups of soup? What if the layoffs come, and our microwave ceases functioning? Are you willing to travel all the way to the floor of the managers to beg for the use of theirs, or shall we starve? These are things to consider, my friend, whether likely or nay."

Bertram the Train-or smiled. "You worry too much. But look, the receptionist doth bring an offering of cake!"

Indeed, the priestess known as the receptionist did enter into the break-room, carrying with her a large sheet cake. The few tribe members present stood or knelt in silent reverence, as she pulled her plastic knife from its sheath and, with deft hands, made the first cuts into cake-flesh. With expert skill, she balanced the sheet cake in the crook of one arm while making her incisions with the opposite hand, until the cake was sectioned into twenty-four neat squares. It was time for the traditional call and response prayer.

"There is cake in the break-room," she droned.

The attending tribe members responded: "Save us a slice."

"It is chocolate, and also vanilla."

"Save us a slice."

"I cut this cake in honor of Caruthers, from Accounting."

"Long may his numbers add up correctly."

"Ensure everyone has a piece before taking seconds."

"Oh, we couldn't possibly."

With that, she carefully lay the sacred knife beside the cake, and produced a stack of paper plates and napkins.

"I did not know we would be taking communion today," mused Wahl'ter.

The tribe of the break-room gathered around their feast and partook. Wahl'ter chose a middle piece, which had cleverly been cut in such a way that there was an edge of chocolate on his vanilla slice. He had always enjoyed marble cake, and thought it represented the duality of his post quite well. His tribe was in a unique position, doing the work of many of the other departments, but having access to so many resources and leisure time. Some outsiders scoffed and said those of the break-room were soft, having been weaned on cupcakes and catered sandwiches, suckling on soda bottles and free coffee and tea. Wahl'ter knew the truth: the additional calories made them strong, and the relaxation their home provided lent them a patient and measured nature, allowing them to strategize and thrive in ways that even the executives envied.

This unique position also made them a target.

No other tribe would be so bold as to attack them outright. There was a carefully curated peace between all the people of the office building, from the top to the bottom. The ecosystem mostly worked, with only occasional conflicts. Still, in the time of layoffs, things could become volatile...

"Good cake, this." Bertram shook Wahl'ter from his reverie.

"Aye, yes," said Wahl'ter. He thought back to the last war over territory. He'd only been a young man when Shipping and Receiving had marched up from the warehouse and demanded fruit pies and crackers. Scant few vending machines lay that far into the bowels of the office building, and their interns would grow weak if not allowed to graze. Words had been exchanged, and had led to a mighty battle between the departments.

The Shipping and Receiving tribe were large and brutish, capable of carrying boxes great distances. They charged upon their forklifts, and only the narrow confines of the elevators, and the rough terrain of the stairwells, kept them from besieging the break-room with their engines of war. Though young, Wahl'ter still remembered the scent of canned air dusters going off, and the whine of the elevators as they strained to carry up an assault force of warehouse grunts. The ingenuity of the leaders had saved them, despite the strength of their enemy. They had retreated to the break-room itself, allowing their workstations and copiers to remain unguarded, and focusing all their defenses around the wealth of resources only the break-room could provide.

When Shipping and Receiving had come calling, a cloud of toner had exploded to obfuscate their vision, then an explosive barrage of rubber band balls, loose paper clips, brads and staples all peppered the invaders until only the screams of the defeated remained. The brutes had not been ready for shrapnel, and even their work gloves provided insufficient armor against the blasts. Never again had anyone tried to assault the break-room. It was too well-guarded, too diligently maintained, and its people too crafty and united to fall.

Still, idly, Wahl'ter touched an old staple scar on his left arm, and wondered when this fragile peace would again be threatened. Layoffs would mean more resources to go around, but unrest and strife often led to furious rage, and that meant supply raiders would be active and numerous.

A sudden ruckus just outside the main break-room caught Wahl'ter's attention. Someone was speaking very loudly. He felt his brow furrow with worry. The break-room was usually a place of quiet contemplation, and excessive noise indicated a growing tension. Too much conflict, and the wraiths of HR would descend to bring order in their own, intimidating ways. Wahl'ter tugged on his tie and went to see what the fuss was about.

"You babble insanity!" Senior Administrative Assistant Jo'see stood over a frightened office drone like a file cabinet of steel, the shoulder pads of her suit jacket flaring up as she prepared for combat.

"I only report that of which they speak! Mercy!" The terrified gofer cowered before her. A group of workers had surrounded the display in a semicircle, using a coffee-break to watch the conflict unfold.

"You came here to bring sustenance, not to spread madness." Jo'see snatched the cardboard tray from the cowering young man, and with deft hands, quickly distributed the chalices to the correct onlookers. "Venti Cappuccino; Grande, Iced, Sugar-Free, Vanilla Latte with Soy Milk; Decaf, Soy Latte with an Extra Shot and Cream; Tall Macchiato with splash of Two-percent. Done."

Although resources were plentiful in the break-room, the roaming office assistants were occasionally corralled to bring messages of great importance to other departments in the far reaches of the building. Sometimes, also cafeteria coffee drinks. This was a useful way to keep tabs on the other tribes without sending spies or disrupting the fragile alliances. These roaming assistants were very useful. It pained Wahl'ter to see one abused in this way.

"Come, Jo'see, surely your ire has been raised without reason. This boy brings us the flavored bean water of stamina; this is a time for celebration and relaxation!" Wahl'ter placed a gentle hand on Jo'see's shoulder pad. He felt it raise and harden under the meat of his palm. He would tread carefully here, lest he invoke her wrath and open himself to power-suit related injury. Worse, he did not wish to be branded a harasser. The break-room had a strict policy of banishment for such cretins.

Growling, Jo'see turned toward Wahl'ter and locked eyes with him. Her piercing gaze caused his spine to shiver, and he felt any more sustained eye contact might rumple his tie with the sheer malevolent energy coming from his colleague. Slowly, Jo'see took a sip of her latte. Tension hung in the air for a long moment, and then, the rage behind her eyes began to subside.

"I had not awoken myself yet today. I apologize. You know I am a bear before my coffee." Jo'see smiled broadly, and Wahl'ter felt himself breathe again. He had seen the transformation of the berserkers before, and Jo'see was one of the most dangerous. Without regular infusions of caffeine, she could easily destroy a normal employee with a barrage of aggression. They were all lucky she was on their side.

"What was the cause of this misunderstanding? An errant reply-all? Could this meeting have been an email?" asked Wahl'ter, straightening his tie.

"This boy brings impossible fantasy. Perhaps he himself is over-caffeinated."

"It's true!" barked the assistant, before cowering again under Jo'see's stern visage.

Wahl'ter turned to the assistant. "What is? Tell me what you've heard."

"M'manager," replied the assistant with a humble bow. "A great discovery has been made on the 20th floor! A miracle thing, beyond dreaming!"

"Tell us of this miracle, then," Wahl'ter said.

"A window!" The assistant's eyes glistened with wetness.

The surrounding members of the tribe chortled, nearly shooting coffee from their noses.

The assistant looked hurt. "I do not lie, m'manager. It has been found just outside the executive elevator! There in the hall, clear as day!"

Wahl'ter Dinsdale studied the young assistant for any signs of deception or intoxication, but found none.

He decided to fish for further clarification. "Do you mean like the windows in the fabled offices of the managers? Those which create a sense of an open office without the need for destruction of walls? Those simply allow the managers to watch over the employees as they go about their business. They are nothing to fear."

"No sir, this window leads to another realm. One where the sun shines, and there is much space, even larger than the whole building!"

"The sun?" chortled one of the onlookers. "The sun is not real! There is nothing outside of the building, fool."

It was true. Nobody had ever seen the sun, except on calendars of beach vacations on the walls of cubicles, and everyone knew vacations were, of course, fantasy stories, meant for entertaining children. The idea that something existed outside the building was amusing as a story, but no more real than any other fairy tale. The scribes who printed the calendars surely had great feats of imagination to share, mighty creative feats indeed, but there was no truth to them.

"Beach vacations are fiction. There is no place where the water cooler has overflowed so far as to fill such a vast concave, and the fine grains of dirt that gleam in the light would be swept up long ago by the custodial staff."

"Sir, I heard the same stories as did we all when I was small, but this seems to be no made up tale. I swear, on the 20th floor, this is all they speak of." The assistant genuflected.

Wahl'ter grimaced as the others continued to laugh. He knew some of the twentieth floor, many of them executives. They would certainly stretch the truth when dealing with other tribes, to greater improve their sacred "bottom line"; however there would be no strategy in revealing such a strange rumor to the rest of the office.

First, rumors of layoffs, and now this strange tale of a window leading to outside? The mind boggled. These were unsettling omens.

Wahl'ter dismissed the assistant, and with the spectacle complete, the other workers of the break-room scattered, all except for Jo'see, who blinked at her colleague as she sipped her elixir. "You look as though you think there is some truth to the assistant's tall tale?"

"I did not rise to the position of master accountant without learning to account for all the facts before making my mind up," said Wahl'ter. "Even if the anomaly is no window, there must be something unusual happening up there for the gossip to reach this far."

The senior administrative assistant grinned, her teeth sharp, honed on a diet of protein-infused milk drinks and hard, vending machine nutrient bars. "You know best, Dinsdale. You know you have my power behind you."

"I pray to the management we need not use it." Wahl'ter frowned.

The afternoon began in earnest, the clocks indicating lunchtime was over and the time for labor had once again arrived. Many would toil from their home cubicle, but only the tribe of the break-room had the freedom to work from computers resting gently upon their laps, perched upon sofas and plastic chairs scattered among the vending machines. The third floor, where they resided, was something of a catch-all, containing a number of middle-management priests and various employees who connected ancestrally to each department. This varied lineage gave them a great deal of flexibility and the ability to problem-solve on the fly.

The sudden loss of connection surprised everyone.

The magical machines used for most of the work in the building were connected through mysterious, invisible rays that traveled through the air like spirits. These connections were maintained by the hermetic artificers of the Information Technology department. The IT area was a dark and isolated place, filled with odd smells and sounds, bizarre contraptions, and a language filled with obscure grammatical constructions and holy words few outsiders could understand.

The artificers mostly kept to themselves, so their attack was completely unexpected.

"I cannot reach the cloud!" cried an intern, pounding furiously at his laptop, trying to make the conduit reconnect.

This exclamation was quickly echoed, as all around the break-room, employees stood, some frozen in panic, others raging and slamming their fists into the desk in frustration.

"My files cannot be updated! I will lose all my work!" cried another, bursting into tears, as the screen before him displayed a series of numbers and letters making patterns of pure gibberish.

A screw flew by Wahl'ter's head as he turned to see the lights dimming, only emergency lights illuminating the space, as even the vending machines flickered like wicked spirits had infested them. He looked up into the nearby air vent to see a pair of glassy, shining eyes dart quickly backward, followed by a loud clattering and an "Ow!"

"Fortify the walls, they're coming out of the walls!" Bertram the Train-or's voice boomed, as he expertly vaulted atop a cola machine and started firing his stapler at the ventilation ducts.

It had to be the IT department. Even now, their tiny mechanical screwdrivers whined and screeched as they fiddled at the corners of the ductwork, trying to gain entry to the break-room's treasures. The IT tribe preferred the darkness, using trickery and subterfuge. Wahl'ter saw it first, near one of the vending machines with the greatest magic of all: The Vend-o-mat. The Vend-o-mat provided hot sandwiches, cold fruit, and even condiment options. These were no mere snacks, but a feast fit for the managers.

Chittering in words only they could understand, two small IT professionals skittered out of one of the overhead ceiling tiles, knocking it to the floor in a puff of asbestos dust. Something glinted in the fluorescence, clutched tightly in the crooked fingers of one of the artificers. Bertram the Train-or was too busy corralling the interns to repel the attack, and in the distance, he could hear Jo'see rampaging with her "coffee klatch crew" through the aisles outside, smashing the IT goblins through desks. One of this tribe was holding two of them under the hot water dispenser, which had been opened to full, while his assistant opened packets of creamer and poured them into the invaders' eyes.

Only Wahl'ter saw the attack was just a distraction so these two could sneak through the security measures, in the darkness like roaches, and access the break-room's stores. The glinting object came into focus as the IT rogue reached down over the front glass of the Vend-o-mat and inserted it into the sacred indentation in the steel plate. It was a universal key, one that would open their vending machines without need for trade or currency. It was a weapon against their very ability to survive.

Sacred mysteries lay behind the machine's ability to re-stock itself with fresh foods and beverages. The tribe of the break-room did not question their gifts from the managers. But, they knew it took time to fully replenish the machine's bounty. If the invaders stole even a portion of their supplies, and the chaos continued to spread, as the rumors indicated, the tribe would go hungry and weaken considerably.

One of the informational technomancers glanced up and saw Wahl'ter staring him down. He squeaked in surprise, and tapped his companion on the shoulder rapidly to indicate they'd been made. The key turned, and the front panel creaked open like the door of an ancient temple. The overhead lights flickered. The managers were angry with this desecration. The thieves didn't care, grabbing up armloads of wrapped sub sandwiches and instant soup cups.

The master accountant could not let this stand.

Vaulting over a rolly-chair, Wahl'ter drew forth his ruler. His hand knew instinctively where to grasp the soft wood, opposite its razor-sharp edge. He felt the joints in his knees strain as he landed, his ceremonial wingtip shoes absorbing some of the pressure, keeping him from tumbling sideways. Channeling his younger warrior days, Wahl'ter leaped toward the quickly retreating IT goblins, who were already scrambling for cover in the air ducts.

He thought back to his training. What were the four steps of the resource acquisition process in resource management?

*Determine required resources.* His eyes focused on those of his enemies, wide with panic and fear.

*Acquire resources.* His blade slashed across the shoulders and chest of the nearest man, tearing his checkered business casual armor asunder. A red spray stained the creature's pocket protector.

*Manage resources.* With his free arm, Wahl'ter Dinsdale reached out and collected as many of the rations as he could, clutching a meal's worth of sandwiches to his chest. They would not hit the dirty tile floor on his watch.

*Control resource usage.* Pushing the dying techno-artificer aside, Wahl'ter slashed at the leg of the other invader, already scrambling up into the air vent.

"No! No! Defiler of the code! Let us go!" came the voice of the thief, a metallic echo.

"Drop the food, nerd-swine!"

The kick surprised him, knocking his tie askew and making him drop several sandwiches. Snorting, the robber disappeared into the ceiling, scratching and clawing his way into the depths of the building.

The sound of robots in great pain broke through the clamor. It was the screeching of the dial-up modem, sounding the retreat. As quickly as they had appeared, the IT department shrank back and disappeared into the darkness, leaving their wounded and dying behind.

"Craven cowards!" spat Bertram the Train-or, leaping to the side of his master accountant. He carried a fistful of pocket protectors - trophies from the battle to add to his already impressive belt.

The break-room was a mess. Here and there, the bodies of the IT department's assault force lay broken and shattered, their PDAs scattered like fragments from an explosion. Valuable rations lay unwrapped, some bitten by those who couldn't afford themselves the patience to return with their spoils.

The tribe of the break-room muttered amongst themselves as they cleaned up the mess, running back and forth, securing the perimeter, checking on the furniture, and reassuring nervous interns. This kind of attack was bizarre, almost unheard of.

While the others went about their business of restoring the tribal fortifications, the elders met around the water cooler. Each took one of the sacred, triangular cups from the ever-filling dispenser and put it to their lips, a silent prayer for peace and clarity of thought. Normally, the water cooler was a place of merriment and camaraderie, but now those below the level of middle management were shuffled away. Fear spread easily, and this conversation would not be easy or comforting.

"Those nerd dogs dare attack our home? We should drive them to the basement to be devoured by the strange machines of the maintenance mages! See if their computer magic works from inside a floor buffer," snarled Jo'see, still raging.

An involuntary shudder went through the group as they imagined being chewed up by the war machines tamed only by the magicians in facilities, the caustic chemicals dissolving flesh, the rotating blade-brushes distributing limbs across a freshly waxed floor.

Bertram brought everyone back to the reality at hand, frowning deeply. "Revenge matters little if we do not survive the time of layoffs. They took supplies, injured our pack of interns, damaged infrastructure. We must focus."

Wahl'ter Dinsdale stared into the middle distance, lost in thought. He silently called out to his ancestors, the first accountants, hoping some advice would come like the flash of a fluorescent light going out, but no words of wisdom came. He glanced around the room, letting the others debate. Vaguely, almost as background noise, like the heating of a coffee pot in the earliest of the morning, his fellows went back and forth about vengeance, fear, starvation. Wahl'ter couldn't let emotions cloud his judgment. He was an accountant. When in doubt, he tried to journey beyond how he felt, and look at the numbers. The numbers would always lead to truth. What were the quantifiable things in this equation?

"My warriors will kill all of them and take their components and build a great metal monument so we never lose connection to the printers again! Their pockets will run with stains of ink and blood!" Jo'see was shaking with fury.

For his part, Bertram the Train-or was standing up to her, though he seemed a bit pale. "Escalate to war? Madness. They would shut down our chat servers, and then how would we play word games together when the TPS reports have stolen our joy? How would we share pictures of cats with humorous captions?"

Nobody had ever seen a cat in the building, but even as creatures of myth and legend, everyone still seemed to be soothed by the presence of artwork involving cats speaking with poor grammar, and sometimes wearing silly costumes.

Wahl'ter stepped between the two warring comrades and held up a hand. Only his position as master accountant saved him from adding more tension to the situation. "Strange omens cannot go unanswered. This talk of a window troubles me. We must go in search of these cursed rumors, even if we find nothing. We will need supplies and information. We have not the wisdom to make these decisions without knowing more."

"Perhaps we should form a committee?" piped up one of the middle managers, his gray pinstriped loincloth flapping as he stood taller.

"No! This cannot be delayed by tradition. I must make … an executive decision." Wahl'ter slipped his pen out of his pocket holster. The tip gleamed as he struck out and slashed it across a nearby white board, spinning it deftly and striking again and again. When the moment was over, the words "AGENDA ITEM: PUT RUMORS TO REST" had been etched in ink.

"You plan to go in search of a window? In the building?" Jo'see scoffed. "Wahl'ter, you venture out in earnest, but your agenda shall become ashes in your mouth. This quest is like a meeting that could have been an email. You'll find nothing, while our enemies grow in strength and number."

"If there is nothing, then there is no danger. You can stay behind if you wish, Jo'see. Perhaps help make the coffee the way people like it." Wahl'ter turned to go.

"I am no receptionist!" Jo'see shouted, then catching herself, cleared her throat. "I shall go with you, if only to be there to laugh when you find these are stories for children. Also, you need protection, for you are over the hill."

Wahl'ter smiled to himself. His friend had fallen into his trap, and she would be needed, as would the intern Train-or. "Bertram, you will come as well?"

"Of course, my friend," Bertram the Train-or said, "You know I shall always be on your subcommittee."

The meeting dispersed as the task force began to gather its supplies. Wahl'ter knew they would need to be well equipped for such a dangerous journey. The 20th floor was no place for the unprepared. However, that meant getting into the supply closet, and to get the key, they would first have to deal with the witches of the secretarial pool.

The climb up the stairwell was arduous. The party linked together long chains of paperclips, at Josee's insistence, in case someone slipped. While the cold air in the shaft chilled them to the bone, the twilight of exit signs and high fluorescents illuminated a vast column of concrete gray ascending ever upward. The elevator would have been a more pleasant journey up the building, but it was too obvious a passage, and their cause would be better served through stealth.

Wahl'ter ran his keycard through the small black box at the side of the door, and the trio slipped silently through the main door to floor fifteen, followed by three interns on neck-tie leashes. This was as high as the stairwell would take them, given the master accountant's security clearance level.

Although on friendly terms with most of the other tribes, the elders of the break-room were wary of the secretaries. Everyone in the building knew to be cautious. Looking at them, most would assume their power was very limited indeed, being physically and departmentally diminutive. Underneath the surface, however, their power throbbed and hummed. The secretaries knew time sorcery, able to know the movements and read the signs of the managers at all times. Some said they even controlled them, working behind the scenes, true puppet masters. They spoke the language of passive aggression, cutting emotionally with blades as sharp as any ruler carried by an accountant's hand. Their ways were mysterious, and so, often, the tribes would sacrifice gifts of flowers and sweet treats to them on their sabbath, the so-called Secretary's Day. Still, one did not want to incur their wrath.

Creeping down the hall of admin wing 15 West, Jo'see held up a hand to stop the others. Sing-song muttering reached their ears.

"Double mocha, creamer, no trouble, coffee percolator bubble!" This was followed by a bone-chilling cackle.

"Hold steady," muttered Jo'see, "These secretaries have strange magic."

Wahl'ter was first around the corner, and he raised his hands to show he was unarmed, holding up his business card as an offer of introduction. "Hail, secretaries. I am —"

"We know who you are, Wahl'ter Dinsdale, and we know why you have come."

An eerie fog settled in, a product of the constantly boiling pots of coffee and tea nearby. Etched into the walls were invocations such as "Think outside the box!" and "Don't reinvent the wheel!"

"Step forward, Wahl'ter, and tell us what you seek."

Three secretaries stood at identical standing desks, situated before triplet computers, typing away. The mechanical keyboards click-clacked a staccato rhythm which danced across the eardrums of those present like ants across a hot metal grate.

As Wahl'ter stepped forward, the overhead lights flashed, and a distant rumbling sound cracked like someone had tipped a whole pile of rolly-chairs on the floors above. "We seek your wisdom, and would ask for the key to the supply closet."

"You seek the key?" one of the secretaries cackled. "You must fill out requisition forms, Wahl'ter Dinsdale, and have them approved by the managers to receive such a boon."

"We are on a great journey and would ask your favor. Simple things, staples, paperclips, sharpened pencils, and the like," Wahl'ter said.

"Do you prepare for battle, accountant?" asked one of the secretaries, stirring the bubbling coffee pot with a tiny wooden stick.

"The journey is long and treacherous! Please, help!" Bertram the Train-or spoke up, lurching forward. "You must assist us!"

The secretaries shot Bertram a look which froze the Train-or in his tracks, all moving together as if one entity. "Do not speak out of turn. You have not been recognized on the agenda." These witches ran meetings with an iron fist, and would brook no rebellion in their territory. One smiled cruelly and gazed upon the trio, who were feeling smaller all the time. "What do you really seek, beyond the key, beyond the closet? Where is your journey's end?"

Wahl'ter clenched his jaw, embarrassed to even repeat the rumor that had brought him here, until finally, he released the tension like the spring. "We seek the window."

"What window?" asked a secretary.

Wahl'ter spoke bravely. "To the outside."

The lights went out.

The darkness suffocated them, embracing them fully. Then, after a moment, the lights flared brightly as a tea kettle started to whistle. The steam now enveloped the area, thick and rich. Wahl'ter couldn't see his companions clearly, their suits and skin only visible in short flashes of motion. He could hear the interns whimpering, with Bertram attempting to find his charges and comfort them.

"Hold steady, hold steady now," came Bertram the Train-or's voice. "Hold! Where are you?"

The laughter of the secretaries hung in the air as the steam cleared, until all three were standing before the heroes, all sipping from mugs. Each mug had a string trailing out, leading to a small paper tag. The pungent brew inside perfumed the air with strong herbal aromas, relaxing the bodies and clouding the minds of the break-room tribe.

"Tea?" asked one of the secretaries. A fresh mug had appeared in her other hand, as if pulled from thin air. Wahl'ter cautiously took it from her and peered into the swirling brown liquid. "Take a sip, you'll like it. Careful though, it's strong."

Wahl'ter brought the cup to his lips and sipped. The spicy, smokey tea hit his palate like a storm. He pulled at the string to remove the tea bag, but to his surprise, the string wasn't tied off with a bag of plant matter, but a small metal key.

"You have what you seek, now go."

Jo'see clamped a strong hand on Wahl'ter's shoulder. "They give up too easily, Wahl'ter; what price would they exact from us?"

One of the women turned her head casually, brushing bangs from her eyes. "We have taken our toll already. Take the stairs, as the elevator is out of service, and smells of body odor." She gestured beyond the large secretarial desk to the central staircase leading up to the executive floors.

"What have you done?" cried Bertram the Train-or. Wahl'ter and Jo'see turned to look, only to see the Train-or frantically opening file cabinets and coat closets. "Where are they?"

"Where are who?" asked one of the secretaries, coolly.

"My interns!" Bertram the Train-or grunted, angrily.

It was true, the trio of interns accompanying the adventurers had vanished. "What is this about?" asked Wahl'ter, drawing his metal-edged ruler.

"A price need be paid, and it has been paid. From where do you think we grow our numbers? Secretary trees?" Now, new laughter joined them, and as they cackled and sipped their cups, three new secretaries stepped from the shadows. They were Bertram the Train-or's interns, now clad in traditional secretary garb: tasteful tops and matching slacks, day-planners clutched beneath their arms.

"Scooter? Skippy? Ms. Thang?" Bertram the Train-or called out, but not even a shadow of recognition crossed the faces of his former proteges. "No!"

"It is too late, Bertram the Train-or. I am sorry," whispered Wahl'ter as his friend held back tears. "Their sacrifice will not be in vain. Come, we must hurry."

As they climbed the stairs to the next floor, the voices of the secretaries echoed in the stairwell. "You shall find your window, but only if you can conquer the obstacles before you. Beware the illusions and tricks of the marketing department, and take care with the wraiths of Human Resources!"

Wahl'ter and Jo'see tried to comfort Bertram the Train-or as they ascended, but his heart was broken. "I trained them from the time they were pups, and their first work-permits were bestowed upon them. They were to blaze new paths."

"Be strong, Bertram the Train-or," grunted Jo'see, "We will need you at full power for the next floor, for you know the supply closet lies beyond the crystal corridors of HR."

The sixteenth floor was beautiful. Fresh looking furniture dotted the lobby, with messages of kindness and work ethic hung on the walls in between as colorful accent pieces. One reading "People with courage and character always seem sinister to the rest." Above, the signature of Hermann Hesse immediately caught the eye, next to sealed glass doors leading into the heart of Human Resources.

Through the glass door, more glass was visible, leading in all directions. A labyrinth of transparency.

"How do we get in?" Jo'see asked, looking for levers or switches.

Wahl'ter turned to Bertram the Train-or, his face an open question. Bertram was lost in thought, barely holding it together. Wahl'ter reached into his pack and removed a box of doughnuts. "Sprinkles. You have suffered a great loss. These will make you feel as if Friday is coming." The leader placed a pink frosted treat in the Train-or's hand.

"Thank you," Bertram said quietly, as he took a bite from the edge, pink frosting spilling from the corners of his mouth. "I'm sorry, yes. The way in. Nobody simply enters HR. They are either summoned, or must discover a wraith with an open door policy."

"Then how will we reach the supplies?" asked Jo'see, tapping the glass.

A quick-moving blur darted across one of the aisles, a streak of black against the shining crystalline glass walls. As quickly as it came, it was gone.

"I do not like this place," said Wahl'ter. "Often, those summoned here with slips of pink are not seen again. It is said this is the last place before one becomes … fired." All three instinctually made the sign of the profits before them, an "S" with two vertical slashes.

"Few enter here willingly," said Bertram, then he paused for a long time. "We must perform a summoning ritual."

"What does this ritual involve?" asked Wahl'ter, adjusting his tie nervously.

"Bah, benefit-bastard magic. I say we smash the door down!" Jo'see grumbled, her shoulder pads flaring like hissing cobras.

"You could try, but that would bring them ever faster. Destruction of corporate property is one of the easiest ways to get their attention." said Bertram.

"Isn't that what we want? To get their attention?" Jo'see retorted.

"We need to be wary of what kind of attention.' answered the Train-or, before sighing resignedly. "Listen, I know what we must do. Follow my directions very carefully. If they smell even a hint of trickery, the summoning will fail."

His two friends gathered closely, as he explained their roles in what was to come.

A few minutes later, Jo'see walked stiffly toward the center of the lobby and cleared her throat. Wahl'ter tried to look busy nearby, leaning against a wall, thumbing through his traveling spreadsheets, which he always carried at his side just in case he had a few minutes idle. Jo'see hummed a dissonant tune and looked around anxiously.

Bertram the Train-or walked up behind Jo'see. The warrior pretended she didn't see her companion, as though he were invisible, even though the hairs on the back of her neck stood on end. Office assistants such as her were well trained to defend against attacks from behind, and stood ready to repel harassers at a moment's notice. This vulnerability felt wrong, and she squirmed in her own skin. Hissing through partly closed lips, she whispered.

"Are you sure about this, Train-or?"

"I am certain."

"But they will mark you. This deed shall be recorded in the permanent file."

"I understand. But I am a Train-or. Only my people are versed in the ancient bylaws of Human Resources. I can navigate their interrogations, at least long enough for you and Wahl'ter to make it to the next stairwell." This was true. As a Train-or, Bertram had memorized tomes of information about everything from the tribal dress codes to the spiritual experiences known as "paid time off".

Jo'see sadly smiled at her friend. "You are a true warrior, Train-or." She closed her eyes, preparing herself, then bent slightly at the hips.

Swallowing hard, Bertram forced himself to pucker his lips into a wolf-whistle shape, and, fighting his every respectful instinct, whistled in the direction of Jo'see. Feigning surprise, she turned, fists up, holding back the desire to punch him in the throat. But, with a warrior's discipline, she played her role to the hilt. "Excuse me, did you just whistle at me?"

Bertram gulped, stood up straight, and looked her in the eye, knowing what was to come. "Yes. I ogled your butt, in the lusty way of our backward forefathers, and now I hereby offer you ..." the wind picked up, as several black streaks flew by the glass, "a promotion ... but only if you will go on a date with me of romantic intention."

"I am a witness," Wahl'ter announced, in his clearest voice, now staring at the interaction before him.

Jo'see recited her lines, grimacing. "Are you saying, on record, you will only help me gain further glory in the eyes of the tribe if I consent to give to you freely of my personal space, body, and sex?"

"I hereby decree it!" said the Train-or, as the air filled with crackling energy, before taking one last look at his friends.

Then with perfect grace, he repeated the steps of the ancient forbidden dance of the harasser, anathema to himself and all modern men of the tribe, knowing it would bring down the wrath of HR upon his brow. He wiggled his hips suggestively, bringing his pelvis forward and back. Next, he waggled his eyebrows three times in rapid succession. Black streams of wraiths were flowing like rivers behind the glass, their howling increasing.

Finally, Bertram bent slightly, stuck his neck out between his raised hands, and went "Brbrbrbrbrb," making a ridiculous sound suggesting he was placing his face between a pair of breasts and letting his jowls flap.

The glass doors burst open with a roar, and suddenly the room was filled with a swirling vortex of wraiths. "Harassment! Sexual harassment!" they cried, as four of them grabbed Bertram the Train-or's limbs and dragged him toward the glass maze.

"Go! Go!" Bertram cried out over the blustering tornado. A gaunt, skeletal face appeared before Wahl'ter, and opened its mouth, a cyclone of echos forming words. "Did you see this man harass his co-worker?"

"Yes," said Wahl'ter, "I shall submit an incident report." The wraith screamed and disappeared back into the swelling black cloud, as another formed in front of Jo'see, who was already running toward the door.

"You will make a statement!" came the voice, like a distant scream from the depths of a cave. Bertram had trained his friend for this moment.

Jo'see leaped through the glass portal and spoke the magic words: "I need to take the rest of the day off to process what happened!" The HR wraith disappeared. Jo'see was on the other side now, but Wahl'ter was still struggling through the churning fog of wraiths, reaching out for her. "Hurry, Wahl'ter!"

"Why do you follow? This is none of your concern!" screeched one of the wraiths.

"I am a witness!" shouted Wahl'ter, as he reached out his hand. The glass doors began to close, and he foresaw the moment where his wrist was sliced through and his appendage separated from his body. At the last moment, Jo'see stretched and grasped the master accountant's hand in her own. She pulled, and with a grunt, Wahl'ter was yanked through just as the doors sealed.

Bertram's face was disappearing into a shadow, and the last thing they saw of him was the whites of his eyes, as he mouthed to them "Go! Go!" The pair quickly ran for the stairwell.

"Hurry, they have puppets!" Jo'see cried.

Wahl'ter looked over his shoulder to see the wraiths holding terrifying effigies of them with button eyes and tiny neckties. Huge mouths appeared in the cloud, hissing the words, "Let's talk about our feelings!" as they pursued their quarry.

Wahl'ter and Jo'see slammed into the stairwell door, ripping it open and clambering through just in time. As they shut it behind them, the tsunami of wraith energy crashed into the door, vibrating the little rectangular window pane. As they hurried up the stairs, they saw emaciated hands holding up paperwork, and as the forms slid down the glass, the words "arbitration policy" were clearly seen before darkness swallowed up the light.

"These stairs go all the way up to the nineteenth level," Wahl'ter said, as he and Jo'see bounded up the stairs. "Then, we need simply walk through marketing, past the board room, to the executive elevator at the end of the hall. It serves only the upper floors, nineteen through twenty-two, so it should be unguarded and easy to enter."

The door was already open when they arrived on the landing of the 19th floor, propped open with a little doorstop and a yellow sign warning of wet floors. The facilities tribe had been here recently.

"Perhaps they are dealing with bathroom maintenance, and will not notice our passing?" Jo'see said hopefully.

"Perhaps," said Wahl'ter quietly. But, he didn't believe they could be so fortunate.

The marketing department felt unreal, a constructed reality. Unlike the other tribes, the marketing people were notoriously deceptive, preferring to use their wily nature to take what the others had worked for as their own. They wove spells of illusion, powered by an unseen force they called "hype", and its chaotic nature made them dangerous to deal with.

"Watch out," said Jo'see, swatting a series of posterboard displays aside. Wild, colorful graphics and charts shot out in every direction, making it hard to know what direction they were facing. "These are meant to confuse us."

"There." Wahl'ter pointed down a small hallway to the side, snaking between cubicles covered in brand logos and dead presentation materials. The word "SUPPLIES" was clearly visible in tight black letters against an off-white, plain looking door. It was the only place on this floor not festooned with slick, colorful fliers and signage.

The pair hurried to the door, and to their great satisfaction, the key worked. Jo'see slapped a lightswitch, illuminating a room with endless shelves. Before them, treasures lay in wait, rows upon rows of regular office supplies like pens and tape, but punctuated by specialty items not seen on the lower floors. They wandered in awe through the room. Here, a mighty paper shredder, an artifact powerful enough to chew up and digest history itself when it was fed paperwork. There, one of the fabled laptops upon which was installed an entire suite of software, so the user could manipulate images and sounds to re-make reality.

Wahl'ter brushed up against a shelf and heard a low rumble. Without warning, Jo'see slammed into him, sending him staggering into a rack of office armor including antiviral face masks, disposable gloves, and fine-quality tissues. She held him against the rack as a shadow loomed, and with a bouncy thump, a giant ball comprised of hundreds, perhaps thousands of rubber bands hit the floor, and sprung away, knocking over a whole stack of sticky notes. "Be on guard, Wahl'ter!" Jo'see lectured.

Grabbing as much as they could, the two quietly stepped back into the hallway. "Does this look right to you?" asked Wahl'ter. The space had shifted. To outsiders, the marketing space was a constantly transforming, ephemeral thing that moved too fast to monitor. Now it seemed like a totally different place than when they'd entered it.

"It knows we're here," Jo'see said.

They made their way slowly back down the hall, but now the graphics and logos were different, and soon they were turned around completely.

"We'll never find this window. We can't even find the stairs," Jo'see growled.

"Wait, I have an idea," said Wahl'ter. He reached into his satchel and plucked the last thing he'd grabbed on the way out of the closet: an economy-sized box of paper clips. "Here, help me."

Together, as they walked, they constructed a metal chain, trailing behind them. It took them what felt like an eternity, but within a few hours, they had a criss-crossed grid of metal wires stretching to the corners of the marketing department.

Wahl'ter thought again of his spreadsheets. Many nights, he had worked long into the time of darkness, trying to get the numbers to add up correctly, or trying to find a flaw in his formulas. "If you eliminate all possibilities, then the only one left must be the correct one." He pointed at the one hallway left without a chain running down and around the corners. To their delight, at the end of the carpet, a bronze elevator stood. Its illuminated buttons with up and down arrows glowed like a beacon.

Suddenly, the noise of a rising number of voices broke the silence.

"What's that?" the pair said in chorus, as they both turned to see one of the office doors opening up. It was the end of a meeting, the worst time to be in the marketing department. Marketing staff poured forth, speaking in their confusing tongue, chattering on about "synergy" and "brand awareness" and "customer acquisition costs." When the group became aware of the two break-room representatives standing in their midst, they stopped promptly.

The largest one stepped forward, holding up a business card. Wahl'ter followed suit, and they snatched each other's cards away to read them over. The marketer squinted. "Wahl'ter Dinsdale of the break-room. I am Matthew of the Key Performance Indicators. What brings you here?"

"We need to use the executive elevator." Wahl'ter replied.

"There is nothing for you above," said Matthew. "Content Ton-eigh, Revenue Rach-el, continuously evaluate the performance of our guests and make adjustments to optimize our marketing strategies." Two of the marketers began furiously taking notes. Wahl'ter noticed several cameras were now pointed in their direction.

"We do not want to disrupt your paradigms," Wahl'ter said, speaking in what he imagined was a marketable vocal cadence. "Only to pass through."

"You can not pass," said Matthew of the Key Performance Indicators. "Your customer journey ends here."

"Customer journey?" asked Jo'see, brashly.

"A framework for a greater philosophy of client nurturing," said Matthew, smiling. "Go back below, to your soft chairs and easy snacks."

"Our journey ends above, at the so-called window. Out of our way," snarled Jo'see.

Immediately, the marketers muttered among themselves, with occasional gasps of surprise.

Matthew looked rattled. "The customer journey is not one-size-fits-all. What the overarching framework will look like depends on numerous factors, including your industry, sales cycle and product or service. But no journey ends with a window. Blasphemy. We will not allow it."

"You are afraid," said Jo'see. "An office manager knows. I can read the mood easily. You fear it may be true, and you fear even more it might be untrue." She stepped forward.

"Throw them into the funnel," Matthew squeaked, "I tire of these debates." The funnel was a metaphor long spoken of in the marketing department, but in this case, they had turned the metaphor into a literal funnel, ferreting employees down a slide and back to the lower floors.

"Wahl'ter, go, I will hold these shallow dolts." Jo'see cracked her knuckles.

"Do A/B split testing and see which half of them is softer!" cried Matthew, taking cover behind the group of marketers. Laser-pointers flashed, blinding Jo'see, as power point slides flew through the air, slashing across her pantsuit and leaving it studded with fuzzy pills and runs. Still, the woman grinned.

"I will show them what happens when customer satisfaction is low," she said, lifting one of the marketers by his lapels and tossing him over a cubicle wall. "Only the office manager can provide you with upward mobility!" She punched two more with a quick combo, sending them flailing into office chairs. "Go, Wahl'ter! I believe in you!"

Wahl'ter ran toward the elevator and smashed his finger into the button.

"Stop him! He will bring down the wrath of the management!" cried Matthew, as a dozen marketers scrambled after the master accountant.

"Come on, come on," Wahl'ter mumbled, as he lit up the number twenty and then repeatedly pressed the door close button. Whispering a prayer to the CFO above, he waved as the doors shut just before the slavering horde reached the elevator. For a tense moment, he wondered who had pressed the button faster, him, the

20, or them, the "up." After what felt like an eternity, he felt movement, and finally, Wahl'ter Dinsdale exhaled.

When the door opened, the ding seemed muted, because there had never been a light like this one. Instead of the cold, white fluorescence of the interior, the hallway was bathed in a warm, golden beam. Wahl'ter turned to look, and his breath caught in his chest.

It was a window.

Five feet tall, with a pane separating the top from the bottom, the transparent glass stood at the end of a small alcove just off the elevator area. Somehow, maybe overnight, it had grown into the building. Surely even now, there were committees being formed, meetings planned, task forces assembled, trying to decide what to do about this object of fear and mystery.

Wahl'ter walked toward it and gazed through it.

The ceiling was endless, a cerulean blue, with white cottony puffs far beyond reach. All around, there were tall buildings, just like Wahl'ter's, other worlds, completely separate from his own. None of them had any windows he could see, but many of them were made from the same materials he was used to. This was a glimpse into what must be infinite alternate worlds, and his knees buckled with the weight of this revelation.

"It is just like in the calendars. How?" he asked himself.

"You came." A deep gravelly voice spoke from behind him.

Wahl'ter turned to face this new threat. He saw a pudgy, rosy-cheeked man, with a beatific smile. "Who are you?"

"I'm the manager, Dinsdale. Well, one of them."

"My manager?" Wahl'ter asked, shocked.

"A manager. I'm not here to stop you. Like you, I was curious."

Wahl'ter didn't know what to say, so he simply turned around and quietly gazed outside again. Strange animals flew through the air, just like in the stories. "Birds," he said, not knowing from where he'd pulled the word.

"Isn't it something? Things are changing. The old ways are obsolete, Dinsdale."

Wahl'ter tapped on the glass. "What's out there?"

"Who knows?" The pudgy man sighed. "I don't. None of us do. I don't think any of us would be able to function out there, in whatever that is."

A small latch had appeared on the horizontal bar in the center of the glass. Wahl'ter flicked it to the side, and pulled up. The window slid open, and both men gasped as the cool air from outside blew across their skin for the first time.

"What are we going to do?" asked Wahl'ter.

"We? Nothing. Most people are too cowardly to try to live any different than the way we're used to. Maybe we should brick it over? You think?"

Wahl'ter thought about his life, about all the things he knew, his attachments and his history. He thought about how his position in the tribe defined his life. It was simply impossible there was something outside of the world he knew, and yet he was looking at it. The wind prickled his skin even as the sun warmed it.

"The managers don't really have a plan, do they?" asked Wahl'ter.

He was met with silence.

Wahl'ter Dindale, master accountant, found himself throwing one leg over the bottom of the window frame.

Outside, his foot met a small ledge. He had never been this high before. Even the balcony overlooking the presentation hall down on second wasn't this high up. He saw the sun, brighter than any bulb he'd ever imagined, and suddenly, he found himself swinging his other leg up and out, and soon, he was sitting on the edge of the window, feeling dizzy, and giddy, and unrestrained.

"You're braver than I, Wahl'ter Dinsdale," came a small voice, but Wahl'ter wasn't paying attention to it.

A bright white light enveloped him, as he stood up on quivering legs, raised his arms, pushed off the wall, and disappeared into the mystery. And, like nobody else in the history of the building, Wahl'ter Dinsdale was flying.

# ABOUT THE AUTHOR

Michael Allen Rose is a writer, musician, and performer based in Chicagoland. He won the 2021 Best Bizarro Novel Wonderland Award for his book *Jurassichrist* and has published with a variety of small presses, writing mostly bizarro, horror, and comedy. He also makes music under the name Flood Damage, and hosts the Ultimate Bizarro Showdown at BizarroCon among other events. He likes tea and cats.

# YOU MIGHT ALSO ENJOY

## CORPORATE CATHARSIS
### THE WORK FROM HOME EDITION

*The pandemic came and the world changed. Lives have changed; work has changed. The boundaries between reality and fantasy have become as blurred as those between life and work.*

## BEST SERVED COLD

by Bob Schoonover

*A dish of corporate greed served with a side of revenge.*

## BUSINESS CARDS

by Laureen Hudson

*If you recognize yourself here, well … I'm sorry about what happened next, but I was on assignment …*

Available in trade paperback and digital editions from
Water Dragon Publishing
*waterdragonpublishing.com*

www.ingramcontent.com/pod-product-compliance
Lightning Source LLC
Chambersburg PA
CBHW030825200726

48288CB00004B/1404